D1008887

TROUBLEMS with FRENEMIES

Pirate Penguin vs Ninja Chicken

by Ray Friesen

Other Books by Ray Friesen

Lookit! A Cheese Related Mishap
Lookit! YARG!
Another Dirt Sandwich
Cupcakes of Doom!
Lookit! Piranha Pancakes

Pirate Penguin Vs Ninja Chicken
Book One: Troublems with Frenemies

www.PiratePenguinVsNinjaChicken.com

ISBN 978-1-60309-071-1
1. Children's Books
2. Pirates / Penguins
3. Graphic Novels

Top Shelf Productions
P.O. Box 1282
Marietta, GA 30061-1282
USA

First Printing, June 2011. Printed in Singapore.

Smooching Consultation: Michelle Harshberger
Legal Services: Benjammin Q. Paddon
Font-ification: Missy Meyer Russian Translation: jJar
Ninjing: Mike Scrase, Ian McMurchill
Coloring Minion: Joe Heath, www.MintyPineapple.com

Edited by Chris Staros & Brett Warnock

What are you still doing here?
Go read the comics!

PIRATE PENGUIN
VERSUS
NINJA CHICKEN
#1
Smoothies and Scuffling
So, um... Why, are we 'versus' each other?
I'm not even mad at you.

AR... That be a toughie. But, a logo's a logo. LET'S GET A-BRAWLIN'!
Or-- we could just go get a smoothie together instead...?
SMOOTHIES!
FRIENDS!

SLURRP!
SMOOTHIE STEVE
Oh, D'you mind paying for these? I left my wallet in my other ninja pajamas.
GRRRR!

Aieee!
Rowr
Erg.
Time out for smoothies.
SLURRRRRRRRRP!

I think I have yours.
WASABI BERRY BLAST
TROPICAL GROG FISH

hee hee hee.
SLURRP!
SLURRP!
Um, hey!

How dare you get penguin spit all up in my smoothie!?!
IT'S ON!
Rowr
Aieee!
THEND

PET STORE
Peer Pressure!
So... I'm thinking about getting a parrot.
Why?
All the cool pirates are doing it.
If all the cool pirates jumped off a bridge. would you, etcetera?
:snort.: Pirates HATE bridges. Don't be a doofus.
I'm not! You--! Shut up.
Snif.
Sigh. Do you wanna come with me to the pet store or not?
YAY!
PET STORE!
14 MINUTES LATER:
BWARK!
YIP!
STEVE'S PET'S

Ow. Dis Barrod id biding by dose.
HeeHeeHee!
This puppy is a licking puppy!
LIK LIKLIK

GLOM!
MINE! I call the puppy. You can have the stupid parrot.
HEY!

What sort of ninja has a parrot? It feels all weird.
All the other ninjas will laugh at me.

I'm laughing at you right now! HAHAHAHAH!
Although part of that is because the puppy is tickling me.

GIMME MY PUPPY!
No! I don't wanna.

THEND

BRAWK!
YIP!
BRAWK!
flap
flap!
Oh, hi! Where are we going? Some place fun I hope!
I hear Super Candy Adventure Island is nice this time of year...

Sticks and Stones and Sugar and Spice
So... um... Are you a boy ninja, or a girl ninja?
WHAT? What kind of question is that?
Well, I was thinking about it -- You're 'Ninja Chicken' not 'Ninja Rooster'. PLUS, you reeeally like candles, scented soaps and stuff.
I have NEVER been more insulted in my LIFE!

What about the time I called you a giant
with extra cheese?
Yeah... that did hurt my feelings kinda alot.
And I'd like to clarify, being called the wrong gender isn't an INSULT, it's merely the inaccuracy that bothers me.
RAWR!

Why aren't you fighting back?

I'm not supposed to hit ladies. My mommy said so.

But surely ladies are allowed to hit other ladies!
Whu? Kuh? Cha!? I HAVE A BEARD!

Yeah, but you could just be a REALLY UGLY Woman!
hee hee hee.
Did I make you angry enough? Ready to fight now?

Aw... There, there.
Snif.
Booooo... Hoooo! Hoo.
THEND

SHINY POWER COSTS EXTRA
YARG!
AUGH!

Woog! You nearly gave me a heart attack!
And you made me drop my sea urchin sandwich...

There'll be time for heart attacks later! Right now, get your sword, we gonna have a duel!
I been practicing my fancy feet works. Hoo ha!

Um... I don't have a sword. My fingers are deadly weapons.

Wanna thumb wrestle?

Um... Not really.
I don't have enough thumbs.

STEVE'S SWORD STORE

Ooh! Nunchuks!

WHEEEEEEEEEEEE!
BONK!

Oog. I don't like nunchuks. They make my face all hurty.
Buy this shiny one! It's more expensive since it's all mystical.

I was thinking this katana set is my style. More Japanesey, ya know? I just worry it's too samurai-ish. Ninjas hate those guys.

No! Buy this one! Just look how glowy it is!
I DON'T WANNA!

Rawr!
HAIYA!

SNAP!

Um, you know, maybe you should buy THOSE swords after all.
Heh heh. I don't actually have any money.

Let's set these down on the floor and run away.
Yes, let's.

THEND

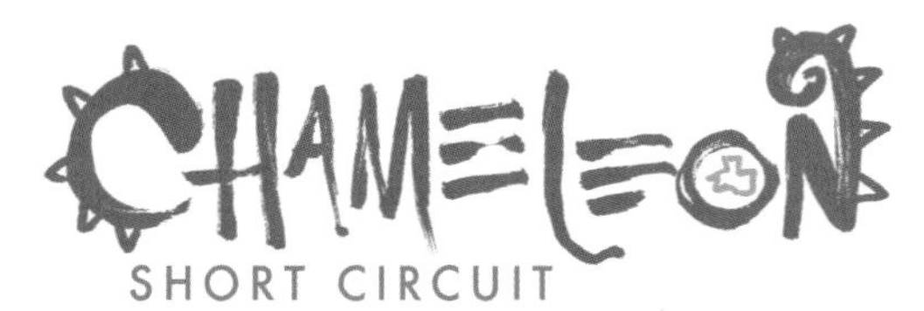

There's something different about you today...

Nuh uh! There's something exactly the same about me today!

NERVOUSNESS!

ALRIGHT, I ADMIT IT! I'M AN IMPOSTER!

I'm a chameleon imitating Pirate Penguin. this is what I really look like.

Wow! That was completely unexpected! You are an EXCELLENT master of disguise!
I know, right?

So where's the REAL Pirate Penguin? Is he okay?
He's all tied up at the moment. I thought I'd keep you company disguised as him.

CHOOoo CHOoo!
HELLO! Ninja? Somebody? A weird lizard guy captured me and stole my hat! HELP!
I'm allergic to getting squished by trains.
THEND

QUESTION INQUIZITION
Can I ask you a question?
Sure! My answer is 'seven!'

Um, it's not a math question.
Okay, then I change my answer to 'yellow.'
Stop answering before I ask! It's making me cranky.

It's more faster. I'm not really interested in any thing you have to say.

You could at least PRETEND to be interested.
Fine. But you owe me one.

Sigh. One what? What do you want?
Hee hee. You fell for it. I would like the following things!

Several Demands Later:
Ahhhhhh. This is the life. Could you rub my feet counterclockwise instead?
RUB RUB
Your feet smell like death. Can I ask my question now?
Actually, I'd like to ask YOU a question first: Why does your voice sound so weird? What accent is that?
Nom Nom Nom
What? I don't have an accent! My voice isn't silly!
If you say so.
HEE HEE HEE
RRRAH!!
YOU'RE MEAN!
THROW!
?
I just wanted to know why you wear a belt when you don't have any pants! Sheesh!
I... I don't know...
Go away, I have to think about this...
THE END

SELFISH SHELLFISH

YAAAH!
I've been practicing the Wakizashi Finger Grip. Let's fight so I can show off my skills!

Nope. We're going grocery shopping.

That's the worst smack talk I've ever heard.

So what are we doing here at Steve's Grocery-atorium? We already have enough mayonnaise and peanut butter.
I thought I'd cook my famous Lobster Hot Dogs tonight.

Ooh! That sounds lovely!
Great! You go find all the ingredients while I stay here in the greeting card aisle and try on sunglasses. Meet you in the seafood section.

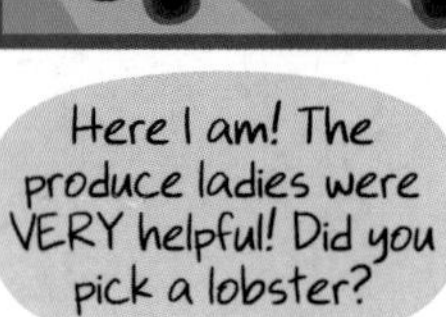
Here I am! The produce ladies were VERY helpful! Did you pick a lobster?

No, I can't decide. They're all tempting me with their deliciousness.

Do you think the manager would let us make them fight, and we could buy the winner?

*Translated from LobsterLanguage
So what do you think, should we break these rubberbands and pinch this obnoxious guy?
Are we allowed to do that?
Hmm... Only if he taps on the glass.
TAP. TAP. TAP.

LOBSTERS! ASSEMBLE! ATTACK FORMATION DELTA!
SEAFOOD FIGHT!
Get 'em off me! Gettemoffme! Getmoffmee! Gofmee! G!
PINCH! PINCH! PINCH! PINCH! PINCH! PINCH! PINCH! PINCH! PINCH!
Wakizashi Finger Grip

Oooooog. Ouch. Ow. I think they stole my car keys, that's why they made a break for it. Owie.
Let's just have this can of soup for dinner.

That's a can of cat food.
Let's just have this can of cat food for dinner.

THE END

Ninja Chicken ALL ALONE
Gimme back my yoyo! I need it for when I perform rap songs so that they'll be accurate!
Hee hee. NO! Why do you think I stole it?

HAIYA! Prepare for--
Oh, crunch! I'M LATE!

Seeyalaterbyeee!
Where you going?

Can I come with?
NO!

So, I'll just stay here all by myself then.

Stupid Yoyo.

Why does it say 'retail price $2.95'? Plus, on the inside someone wrote "Dear Mrs. Nesbit, sorry I broke your toaster."

It's preprinted. Must be a typo.

FINE. Here's your money. So, what present did you buy for Astronaut Armadillo?

I got him one of those combination yoyos/cell phones!
Ooh! I think I'll be needing one of those!

They were 'buy one get one free' so... I picked you up one.

Aww! You're the best Pirate Penguin ever!
Augh! What are you doing? Stop ruining the moment with hugging! It makes me throw up!
Hugz!
THEND

BONUS WISDOM!
ASTRONAUT ARMADILLO SEZ:
Hey kids! Eat your friggin' vegetables!

Follicle Follies
Hey Ninj-- D'you think I should shave off my beard?
Yesperately!
I'm being serious.
I'm not. I'm being very silly today.
Cuz, y'see, with my beard, I'm more fearsome and piratey...
I'm usually pretty levelheaded, what's gotten into me today? Oh that's right, I'm loopy from all the sugar I ate. Stupid delicious Ninja-Candy.
... But without it, I'm much more cute and merchandisable.
What? Ew! Gross! How are you doing that?
Secret Flabby Folding Powers.

So, what do you think, Yes or No?
Oh, jeez um, Yes?

Great! I'll go get the hot wax and sharp things.
Okey-dokey! I'll stay here and guard the universe.

Waitaminit... What? I wish I remembered what his question was so I would know what my answer meant.
I'm kinda scared.
CLIPPEDY! CLIP! SNIP! VWIP! WIP!

17 NOISES LATER...
HALT! Who goes there?
UN-HALT! Me! I goes wherever I wants!

So, whaddaya think?
Oh! You... shaved your beard? Well, um, it looks...
I know, I hate it too. Help me glue the clippings back on.

How do you think I'd look with a beard? They're hard for us birds to grow.
Hey! That's my beard! Gimme!
Or howzabout a moustache?
You don't have a nose! You look weird and also stupid!
Oooh! I'm angry at you!
Hee hee hee!
Rar!
No, I'm very angry with you.
Okay, I had my fun. Gee you're heavy.
Fatness Powers. Now, gluey gluey! Be a dear and help me put my face on.
SMEERP!
So, how do I look?
Less ugly than usual!
THEND

ARACHNOPHOBIA
So... bored...
And that's how I KNEW the kitten was up to no good!
EEEK!
Hey, no screaming - yet! I haven't gotten to the scary part with the tap dancing ghosts!
And now you're cowering behind me.
Sp...! It's a sp...! Spuh...!
What is it? Spies? Ninja Spies?! Ninja Spy Assassins after all my secret documents?!? I hate those guys!
It's a... spider!
Icky!
glare
Wuss.
flik
Ow!

I'm sorry, I've just always been scared of spiders. Long ago, when I was a lil ninja back at my grandma's house in Japan, we got attacked by a huge spider monster. I was slightly traumatized!

That didn't happen. That was a movie. Godzilla destroyed the spider at the end. And the people of Tokyo lived happily ever after.
Yeah, but I WATCHED that movie at my grandma's house and got all scared. PLUS she made me eat liver and onions, and that was scary too.

Just, get rid of the spider. Please? As a personal favor to me?

My personal favors cost cash money.
Here's my wallet. Take a dollar out.

Yes. ONE Dollar is the amount that I'm taking out...

Hullo everyone! My name is Myron and I'm here to--

SWONK!

Goog.

AUGH! I meant scoop it up in a jar and release it into the wild!

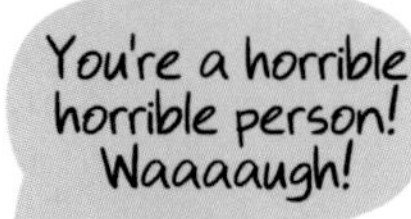
You're a horrible horrible person! Waaaaugh!

Pirate Penguin in: Untitled

Sorry Chicken, I can't 'versus' you today. I have a SPLITTING Headache.
Awww! I'm in a really fighty mood right now!

Yeah, well, I just wouldn't be able to beat you up as soundly as normal, it wouldn't be fair to you...
That's okay, I'll just call one of my other martial arts friends... Hello, Kung Fu Koala?
SPARRING PARTNER ROLODEX

What? Hey! Don't you even wanna know HOW I hurt my head?
Not really.
DINKLY DONK!
Greetings, Honorable Master.
Mrnk.

KREEGAH!
Would you like some tea before--
SPOONK!

Hey, no fair! I wasn't ready!
Bwak!

See, HERE'S how I got my headache: I was teaching myself to juggle, like so--
Fling!
KLOONK!
Hey! My headache's gone! Fight fire with fire!
KLOONK!
Oh, wait. Nope. It's back. Hello, my excruciating friend.
Meanwhile, at the fighting:
Ow! Ow! Ow! Ow! Ow! Ow!
CHOMP! CHOMP!
This is painful.
KLOONK!
Pirate Penguin! You saved me! How can I repay you?
With money?
No. How else?

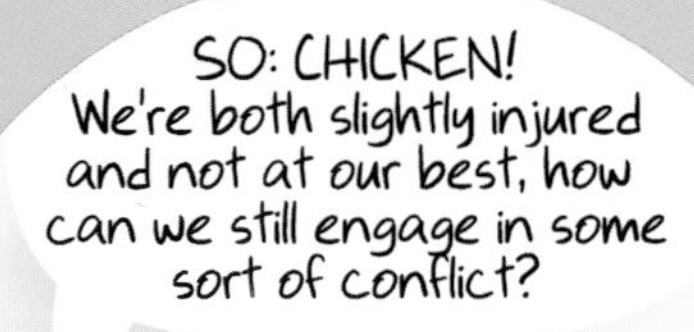

I forget some of the rules... This horsey guy moves in a R shape, right?

That's a Knight. He moves in an L.

I'm going to move him in a Q shape. Q's are cooler.

White always goes first. Do you even know the rules?

THE END

Quick! Everybody DISCO!
Nope. Reading Sun Tsu's 'Art Of War.'
Hoo Ha Hoo! Dibbedy Dee!
Come on Chicken! Dance with me!

I'm too busy ignoring you.
You're BOOOORING.
Yes, but I am very well-versed in Battle Tactics.
YOINK!
Yes, but are you well-versed in Beanbag Chair Tactics?
HEY! I need that to be comfortable!

To get your beanbag chair back, you have to put down that stupid 'Arts and Crafts of War' book, and show me your disco dance moves!
POKE!
Um... I think I spilled the beans.
BOONK!
pirouette!
un consciousness!
Hee hee.
Ooh! Penguin's comfier than the beanbag!
MAORI
HAKKA
CHAPTER 7
BATTLE DANCES
STRIKE FEAR INTO THEIR HEARTS WITH A FEARSOME DISPLAY
THE END

BREAKFAST of CHAMPIONS
Hwonk... Shu. zzzZZZzzZz
Ninja Chicken? Are you awake? Hey. Psst! Ninja?
NINJA CHICKEN! WAKE UP!
ZzzSnork... Huh?!?AUGH! Release the Tigers!
What? You don't have any tigers, do you?
YAWN? Haha! No, of course not. That was... leftover dream talk.
GRRR!
Shh! Quiet, Toni!
CLOSET
Hey! Pirate Penguin!?! What are you doing in my house? It's the middle of the night!
TECHNICALLY, it's the middle of the very early morning. And this is OUR house! We're room-mates!
What? We are? No we're not! Since when?
Oh yeah, I forgot to tell you. I needed a place to crash, my house was too dirty. I snuck all my stuff in a couple weeks ago.
How did you manage to sneak past me, an almost fully trained NINJA?
SHEER AWESOME-NESS! Also, I'm wearing socks.

Okay, so, you've woken me up. What can I do for you?
Well, I was making myself a nice Midnight Mochaccino to start the day off right, when accidentally...
BLENDCO
FVIVRIRIR!
FVIVRIRIR!
FVIVRIRIR!
Nom nom nom.
So, would you mind fixing... Y'know, everything?
Why didn't you just use the Coffee Machine?!?
WOO! WOO!
We have a Coffee Machine? Oh good, the fire department's here...
THEND

TOUGH Yet FLUFFY

Oops.
You know you're not supposed to hang out with those nasty Campfire Raccoons. They're a bad influence on you.
Yep!

Were there... SING-ALONGS?

Just a few tiny ones. You wouldn't have known the words anyway.

I am so upset, I'm not even able to face in your direction.
I brought you a leftover magic marshmallow!

I don't want it. It'll turn me all funny looking like you.
Hey! I'm dashingly handsome, my mommy said so.

Besides, it's probably only leftover because you dropped it in the dirt.
Nu uh! I dropped it in the sand...

Toss!
Well!

Goonk!
Magic!
I am going to knock the stuffing out of you!
THEND

NIGHT FIGHT
Okay, my blindfold is all secured. Now what happens?
FWINK!
FWINK!
FWINK!
FWINK!
FWINK!
What was that fwinking noise?

Shurry-urken! I'm practicing throwing ninja slicey stars at you!
What?! I thought we were playing 'pin-the-tail-on-the-thing-that-needs-a-tail!' Why are YOU blindfolded?

Because I'm also practicing BEING AWESOME!

Now, hold still.
Yes, holding still. That is what I will do...

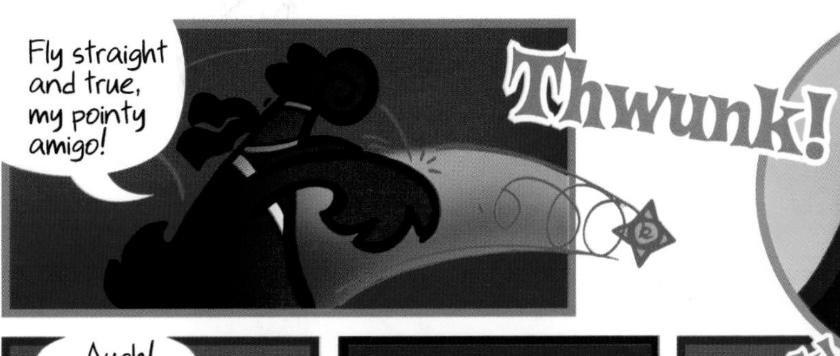
Fly straight and true, my pointy amigo!
Thwunk!

Augh! PP! Are you okay?

PIRATE PENGUIN

Thwunk!
Where'd you go...? huh?

I thought I'd fight back. Leave the blindfold on.

Hey! That's not fair!

Who said I wanted this to be a fair fight? Well, in that case...

Click

Okay, that was our BEST FIGHT SEQUENCE EVER! I wish I could have seen it.

THEND

Hey! Does you wants some bubbled-gum?
Since when do ninjas chew gum?
Since Septembuary.
Bubble TROUBLEMS
Hmm. What flavor is it?
Pinky sugarish.
Mmm... No. Do you have any peanut butter? Or jellyfish?
Please just accept my generous generosity.
FINE!
Ernk.
Lil bit
Just gotta!
Got it!
Onk!
Foomp.
Ark!

Opening gum with a hook looks impossiblish! How did you lose your flipper tip? Why do you have a hook for a hand?
I told you before: It's a secret mystery, that I can only reveal on my deathbed!
What if I guess? Did it happen like...this?
No.
TUNA
Did it happen like this?
Is that an alligator or a crocodile?
Croc.
Then No.
RAWR
Howzabout like this?
N...Maybe. That would be pretty awesome, tell every-body that.
Liar.
ARG! I've been in way more fights than you, and have not lost a single body part! You're just careless.
I can't tell you about my hand, but I will reveal the secret behind one of my other missing body parts...
WINK!
THEND

REVENGE! The Musical
Grr! Arg! Rasser Frassin Stupid Dry Cleaners. Grumble Mumble!
Hello Piratey Penguin! Sup?
I can't exchange pleasantries with you Ninja Chicken! Don't you see what has happened to my beautiful hat?
It's looking a bit more crumpledy than usual.
'Zactly!
So hey-- Notice anything different about me today?
I don't have time to notice things, I'm sure you look more exactly the same than ever before.
Really? Look closely, there are several--
Zip it! We have some destruction to do to a certain Dry Cleaners. Pickup that flame thrower.
Ooh, um, well, nervousness!
Astronaut Armadillo Sez!
Hey Kids! Arson is never the answer! Name calling is just as fun, and brings way less prison time!

REVENGE! Revenge against stupid dry cleaners!
I'm fairly certain this contravenes several city ordinances.
STEVE'S CLEENING

Drat, he's closed for lunch. We'll have to hang out for a bit. I'll downshift my rage to 'simmering'.

Hey guys, what is the up?
SLURP!
SLUUURP!
Augh! The Real Ninja Chicken! I mean, um, also me! Hello! I am you from the FUTURE! WoooOOooo!
Nice try Camouflagey Chameleon, I totally know it's you. The belt is a dead giveaway. Why do you keep using your shape shifting powers to try and trick us? It's weird.

SHOONK!
TRANSFOOOORM!
It's mostly boredom, plus loneliness and hero worship.

Steve The Owl The Dry Cleaner! I've come for my REVENGE!
Do you have a receipt?
CHOMP CRUNCH

Evil Cleaning Monster! My hat has become far too crinkly in your clumsy hands, and that makes me cranky!
I think it looks cool that way. You could set a trend. A trendy trend.
ARG! Violence!
Okay, okay...
Hey, Ninja Chicken. So, he says I can come back for my revenge on Thursday. He gave me this loaner hat from his pirate stash till then. You've got to admire his evilness.

Hey! Green dude! Do I know you? Didn't you tie me to some railroad tracks that one time?

Um! Maybe! I don't, -- HEY WHAT'S THAT OVER THERE?
Huh?

FWOOSH CHANGE!
Now! To answer your previous question: No, I am very obviously a different guy from that green guy you thought I was. Lookit, see?
Woah, that thing over there! It's so beautiful!
What is it? Some kind of Mystery Thing?
Uh, guys?
THEND

Pirate Penguin Vs Ninja Chicken: Card Trick or Treat

FLOMP

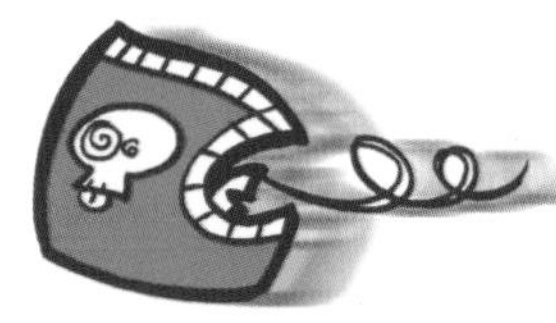

floonch!

RiP!

ROUND 3
KLOONK!
?
gloo
gloo
Thend.

THE BIGGEST! GIANTEST EPICEST PIRATE PENGUIN VERSUS NINJA CHICKEN STORY EVAR!!

o my G!

PART ONE: breakfast

Sigh. I hate waiting for things. Hate it SO MUCH.
tap tappedy tap

If only I knew how to tell time, I could complain MORE SPECIFICALLY.

Waitaminit... Since when do I wear a watch?

Weird...

What?!? You didn't tell me that! I can't wait **6 days** to eat my cereal! It loses its zestyness after 4!

I told you I was leaving every day for the past week. Everybody threw me a 'going away' party last night.

I really don't think you've thought this whole 'going out of town' thing through. Who will cook for me? I'll starve.

I filled up the fridge with groceries. Fend for yourself.

All I see is raw vegetables and ingredient-type thingies. No actual FOOD food.

Eating a stick of celery won't kill you.

It might. What if it's poison celery? Or the exploding kind? Or just icky?

OmyG! This is your secret plan to assassinate me!

Pirate Penguin! If I wanted you dead, I would have assassinated you YEARS ago.

...Good point. I really appreciate you not killing me so far, by the way.

No probs. You saved my life that one time, so I am honor bound to protect you whenever it doesn't interflict with my schedule.

Oh yeah, I forgot I rescued you! Um... would it make much difference now if I told you it was me that set that bear trap in the first place?

I was stuck in it for four days, I nearly starved to death.

Well, now you know how I feel! Stuck with nothing but celery, honestly! PLUS! Who's gonna read me my bed time story every night? Huh?

XRAY
You know full well I can't do the silly voices.
FINE. I'll call you every evening and read a story to you. Any other troublems?

Any special instructions I should know about feeding the cat?
We don't have a pet cat.
Fine! Then I'm getting a cat just to spite you!
CLICK!

Pirate Penguin? I always wanted a cat, you're the one that's allergic... Hello?
BEEEEP
LAST CALL!

Scuse me sir or ma'am-- please turn your cell phone off before the plane is all up in the sky!

Okay miss.
BOOP
Y'know, I think this trip will be nicer if I keep my cell phone turned off the whole time...

Astronaut Armadillo? The party's over. Please get out of my house. Yarg, I hope he's not dead. NASA'd prolly make me fill out a bunch of paperwork if he died at my house.
ZZZZzzzz Snerk. Wuzzat?

PART TWO: More Breakfast

Urnk. Oh, howdy PP. Food in T minus Ten?
No. Food in Q divided by 37.
What does that even mean?
I don't know. Just go away.

No. TEN! NINE! EIGHT!
What are you--?
SEVEN! FIVE!
Hey, no fair, you're skipping numbers!

THREE! TWO! ...Don't make me say blastoff.
FINE! I'll make you breakfast!
Hee hee. I win!

Yum! Num! Um.. Why are you wearing a chef hat?
Because I own a VERY impressive hat collection, and I don't often get the chance to show it off.

Mmm OJ. Sluuurp.
SPIT SPITTEDY SPIT!

What is the malfunction with this orange juice?
Um, it's the extra pulpy kind?

Fresh Squeezed?!? NONONO. I like the frozen kind! Aged at least two years.

And what is the situation with this cereal?
I make it myself out of bacon and sausage!
MEATY MEATS

A meat cereal? Hmm.. What are these little white bits?
Marsh-mellows. Occasionally bones...
Pass the milk.

We're all out of regular milk, so you'll have to use my **special** kind.
M!

Um... this milk is brown. Is it chocolate, or gravy?

Yes!
Blecch. I can't eat this.
HEY! That's a BUNCH of expensive pork products, you can't just throw it all down the drain!

Speaking of drains, I'm gonna go use your shower. I hope your shampoo is tear-free! Bring me some fresh towels, and have my space suit dry cleaned.
Maaaaaaan! taking care of this dude is annoying! Now I know what Ninja Chicken must feel like taking care of me...

Ugh. I hope this doesn't turn into a learning experience.

PART THREE: Inflight Snack

Rule #1. Everybody be extra safe. Way safer than usual. Seat 5Q- Safen up. Rule #2. No spitting. Rule #3. Seatbelts go around your middle, Seat 5Q, you're doing it ALL wrong. Don't make me come back there.

Now, if the plane crashes at all during the flight, that would be bad. Everybody cross your fingers that it doesn't.

That's our only bag of peanuts, so everybody feel free to fight over it.

Wanna go hide in the back and watch the in-flight movie?

I thought you'd never ask!

PART FOUR: Telephone Call #1

Because I voted NO on the whole Video Phone Idea! I have a lovely speaking voice, and I was totally cool with the old Regular Phone System.

PART FIVE: Walking Calamari

Yes, I am! How could you possibly tell?

I'm secretly a world famous detective. My powers of observation are LEGENDARY.

Okay, yes, I'm dressed in ninja pajamas, you don't hafta get snippy.
Ahem.
WE RESERVE THE RIGHT TO BE SNIPPY

Fair enough, that all seems to be in order... Where was I? Oh yes. I have a room reservation!
Last name?
Chicken.
First name?
Ninja.

Just out of curiosity, what's your middle name?

Sambidextrous!

Hmm. We have seventeen reservations under the name 'Ninja Chicken'.

Fourteen of those are cousins of mine. I dunno who the other three are...
Which Ninja Chicken are you?

The cute one!

Well, it's a moot point anyway. We already ran out of rooms.
MOOT? But I made a reservation!
NO

WE RESERVE THE RIGHT TO BE FRUST RATING

That sign said something different a minute ago...

WE RESERVE THE RIGHT TO ALTER REALITY

What a wierd policy. Are you sure there aren't any rooms left?

Well then, I'd better go stand outside and look dejected.

Ninja Chicken! Is that you?

What? Oh, yes, I am me. Usually. Do I know you?

It's me! Ninja Squid! Remember, we went to Ninja High School together?

Oh, hi? Um, how are you?

Ninjatastic! So, you're staying at this hotel for the convention also?

Well, I was supposed to, but they're all out of rooms...

Gee, that stinks! I have a room, I showed up last week on accident. The Ninja Con hadn't even started, it was a Dental Hygienist Convention. I learned more about teeth than an animal with no teeth should ever know.

But you do have teeth!
Nuh uh.

But--
Oh, these are novelty dentures. I bought them at DentalCon.

See look, I press the button, and, FWING! I'm a vampire!

Oh, that must... come in handy?
Not really. I kinda regret buying them. They were way expensive.

Well, g'bye! I have to try and find a new hotel within walking distance.
You could come stay in my room, I've got a spare bed.

Oh, um, that's really nice, but I don't really know you...

We went to Ninja College together for 17 years!

Are you sure that was me, and not one of my cousins? There are alot of Ninja Chickens y'know...
Nope. Definitely you, you're the cute one.

That's both flattering and creepy.

Thanks! I'm multi-talented! And multi-tentacled.

PART SIX: Sandwich Inna Tube

I'm beginning to see why they might have left you on the moon...
HEY! Hey? Hey. Everyone loves me, I'm a hero!

What heroic things have you ever done?
I'VE BEEN IN SPACE!

That's impressive, sure, but not **heroic.** Have you ever saved a puppy from a burning building? Or saved a building from a burning puppy? Or even defeated a nefarious villian?
I defeated my evil cousin Jimmy in a poker game once. Well, I say defeated... he had better cards, but when he wasn't looking I put a pinecone in his drink!
BLAST-OFF CHAIR

Uh huh. Can you fly?
That's really more of a SUPER hero thing, not--

CAN YOU FLY?

UNCLICKEDY!

WOW!

It's Zero Gravity, ya doofus.

What? Are we in space already?
Duh, for like, 20 minutes now.
Where was the blastoff part?
Count-downs are so 1970s.

Okay... So, what does this button do?
That kills us all horribly.

What about this one?
That kills us all slightly less horribly.

Are all the buttons murdery?
No, this one flushes the Zero G toilets!

PART SEVEN: Telephone Call #2

Okay, you are getting more and more weird...

Yup! So, I was thinking we could stay up till 4a.m. telling knock knock jokes, as well as all our hopes and dreams. I'll probably end up complaining a bunch about my grandmother's poodle, Mrs. Yippy.

This is gonna be the best slumber party EVAR!

Yeeeeeeeeaah, I just remembered, I have to call my frenemy and read him his bedtime story, I'll be out in the hallway.

You can call your friend in here. Dial nine first.

BEEDLE BEEDLE
BEEP BEEPIDY BEEDLE
BEEP
Hey Pirate Penguin, it's me. It's your bedtime, so I thought--
Which me? It's not MY bedtime, it's only 3200 hours o'clock.

I really just wanted to get away from Ninja Squid, I-- wait, what? Why are you talking in military time? It's dark outside, time for bed!
Ha ha ha! Oh you silly landlubber. It's always dark in the void of space! I'm in orbit around Norway, and it's technically lunchtime there, so--
DANGER
UK

Mmm! Zesty!
SPRITZ!

What are you talking about? Where are you?

I'm at the wheel of a space shuttle. Astronaut Armadillo stepped outside for a minute, he doesn't trust the Zero G toilet.

Are you **seriously** trying to tell me you're in outer space?

No, I'm in a ship that's in space. And technically, it's not even outer space, it's the ionosphere. Read a book.

It takes years of training to become an astronaut!

Apparently not. Astrodillo's uncle is a senator or something. That's how he got in. Plus, it's 'take your buddy to work' day. Those astrophysicists are pretty cool once you get to know them! Well, most of them...

You liar! How can you look me in the eye over the phone and lie to me like that!

Don't believe me? I'll send you a pic!
PCHIK!
SEND!

Woah. I'd claim that was photoshopped, but I know you don't have the computer skills.

What? That's what Tech Support told me to do.
4 0 4
See? You're not the ONLY person who can go out of town unexpectedly! Jealous?
Totally!

How are you even getting cell phone reception in space?

Ninja Chicken, all the satellites are up here. I've got 17 bars.
CELL-U-COM
So what's you guyses Space-Mission?
I dunno. Hold on, I'll find out--
UNWIND
UNWIND
UNWIND

Augh! Close that window, you're letting all the space in!
I don't even know why we have these kind of windows. Now, what did you need?

Your fly's unzipped.
So, what's our mission supposed to be?

It's Wednesday, so we're bringing a fresh batch of comic books to the International Space Station.

NC, I gotta go. Comic books.

Are you done? I've set the microwave on fire, so we can make smores!
CLICK!
BEEEEEEEEEP!
I can't wait for it to be tommorrow allready...

PART EIGHT: One Long Night Later
Wakey wakey! Eggs and Bacony?
One Breakfast Later:
Buffet
MmmMM! I love pamcakes, especially when they're waffle shaped.
Are you ready to get our Con on?
You know it!
SQUID
NINJA

NEAKY
Whoa. This is way more fightingey than I was expecting... and pitch dark.
You know how ninjas are.
So, what, is it like, last ninja standing gets a prize?
I sure hope so!
If it comes down to just us as the final two, will you go easy on me?
I can't make that promise. HAIYAH!

Sure! I've got more enchanted cutlery if ya want: The Golden Tea Spoon of Lightning Energy? The Lost Fork of Poseidon?

LIKE NEW

Just the sword please. Here's my credit card.

STEEV'S SWORD EMPORIUM
OWNER/OPERATOR OWL
Can I see some ID?
Nope.

Why not?
Um, I'm a master of disguise. My ID wouldn't be any good anyway.
YOYO of DEATH

Eavesdropping! I'm a master of disguise too! Let's be friends!

Get away from me, you weirdo!
Okay. I don't want to be friends with some-one who'd hurt my feelings so much anyway. Snif.

I must insist on seeing some identification.
FINE! HERE YOU GO.
DO AS HE SEZ

This is a library card. I need Photo ID.

SCRIBBLE
SCRIBBLE
SCRABBLE
Ta da!

Whatever. It's not as if I follow all those law thingies anyway. Here you go. Pleasure doing business with you.
Yes, I'm a very pleasant person.
STEEV'S SWORD EMPORIUM

MwahHee HeeHeeHee!
Scamper Scamper Scamp

Psst! I think he was lying about being a pleasant person.

Yes, he did mention that he was evil earlier, actually. I better take a look at the prophecy chapter from the Encylopedia of Wisdom...

OH MY.
ENCYCLOPEDIA OF WISDOM

WHAT? What is it?
I'll tell you for ten dollars.

PART NINE: Fancy Space Chocolates

What? What is it? Space aliens? Awesome! If it's a fight they want, I'll give it to them! Charge the laser cannons! Arm the proton torpedoes! Hoist the mizzen mast, splice the mainbrace! Oops... I slipped from space-ical into nautical. My bad.
It's not space aliens.
Aw man.
It's something... MUCH WORSE.
Yay! I'll bust out the battle champagne and celebratory fancy space chocolates!
No, this fight is for me alone. You see... IT'S MY ARCHNEMESIS.
You mean...?
YES.

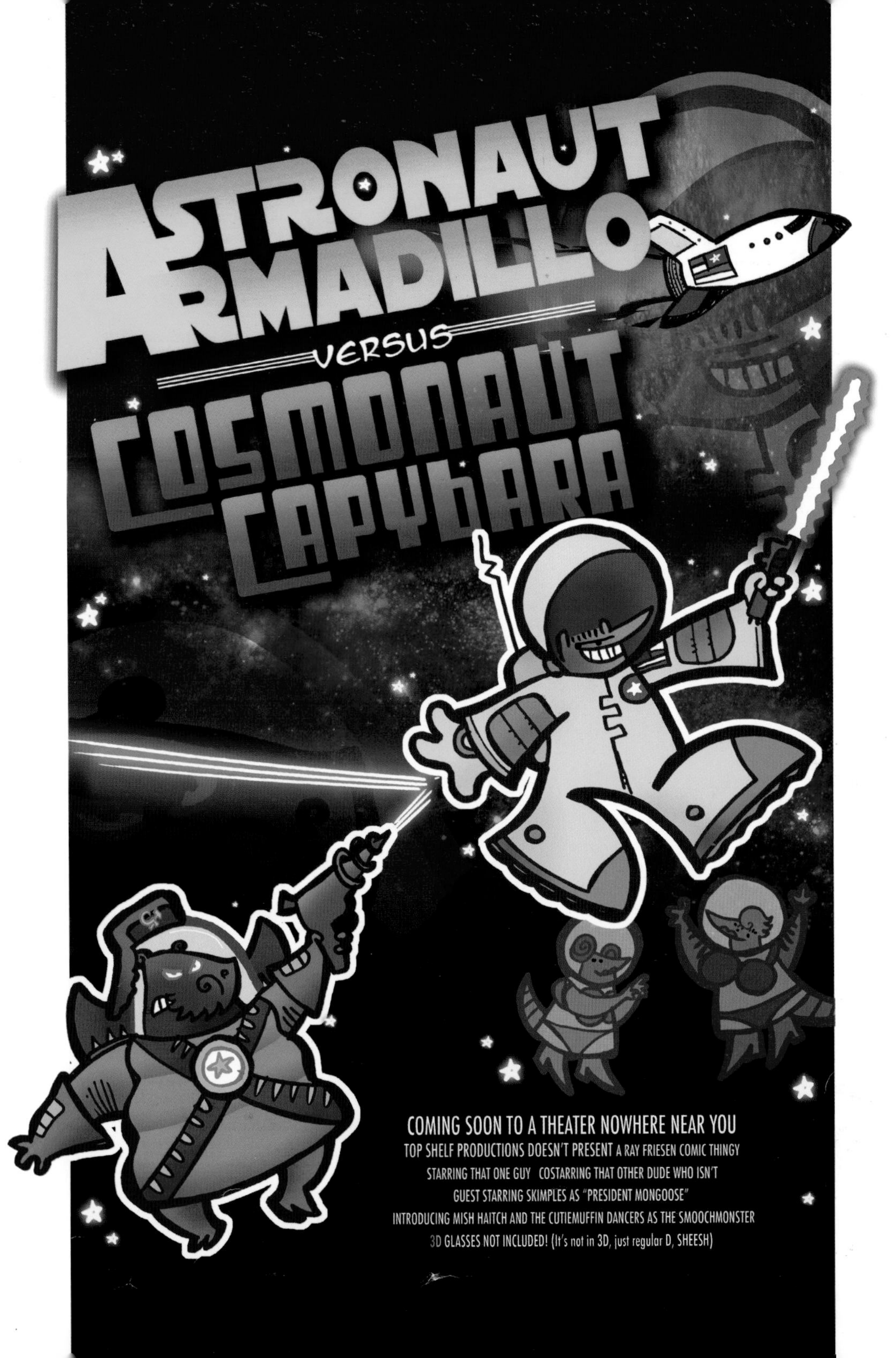
ASTRONAUT ARMADILLO
VERSUS
COSMONAUT CAPYBARA
COMING SOON TO A THEATER NOWHERE NEAR YOU
TOP SHELF PRODUCTIONS DOESN'T PRESENT A RAY FRIESEN COMIC THINGY
STARRING THAT ONE GUY COSTARRING THAT OTHER DUDE WHO ISN'T
GUEST STARRING SKIMPLES AS "PRESIDENT MONGOOSE"
INTRODUCING MISH HAITCH AND THE CUTIEMUFFIN DANCERS AS THE SMOOCHMONSTER
3D GLASSES NOT INCLUDED! (It's not in 3D, just regular D, SHEESH)

Well... good luck with that.
I don't need luck! I just need bravery... heroism... truth, justice, honesty, a nice haircut, the good old Red, White and Blue, a bit of luck, and of course, oxygen.

Oh, and could I borrow your sword?
Sure.

To insanity, and beyond!

COSMONAUT CAPYBARA, you jerk! You never gave me back my Moonicorn Princess DVDs!

Tovarishch, v cosmose zvuk otsutstvuet. Ya tebia ne slishu! Otprav' mne textovoe soobshchenie! Znaesh' moy noviy nomer mobilnika?
*There is no sound in space comrade, I can't hear you! Send me a txt message! Do you have my new cell phone number?

...What?

PART TEN: Koala Kandy

BEHOLD! The key to your destruction!

Well, it's really more a sword than a key... It's a metaphorical key, y'know?

You're not even paying attention to me, are you?!?
I think they're kinda distracted.

Fine. Never mind! Sure I spent ALL NIGHT writing this victory speech, but who cares?
What are you doing?
EVIL SPEECH
Drawing secret symbols.
Why?
STAB
To open up a mystical gateway.
And?

Release a giant monster! Duh!

Rawr.
ptui!
Hoo hoo ho haha haha ha hee hehe!

gasp!
gasp!
snork!
gasp!
gasp!
gasp!

Okay! I'm gonna go on a rampage now. Any of you ninjas wanna come with?

PART ELEVEN: Land Ho!

Can't believe they were hundreds of copies of the SAME COMIC BOOK. Good thing I have a TeeVee or I'd be totally bored right now.

HAIYAH!
Um, hey, Ninja Chicken?
Oh, Hi Camoflaugey Chameleon. Nice to seeya again -- I'm kinda busy right now, heroically fighting against overwhelming odds.

Yeah, I noticed. I had an idea-- that nasty koala guy used this mystical sword of shiny power to conjure the monster. Maybe YOU could use the sword to unconjure it?

OFFICIAL

You think maybe that's the monster's achilles heel or something?

Did you drag that podium all the way out here yourself? You're strong!

OFFICIAL PODIUM

Now, I just need something to distract the monster so I can get close enough...
Hey, what's that up in the sky? It's a bird. It's a plane!

It's a bird in a plane...

It's... PIRATE PENGUIN! Dunt da da dah!

BOONK!

OW! That Really, REALLY hurt! What is wrong with you?

Now I have the biggest headache EVER! I better take some aspirin.
PHARMACY

HAI YAH!

GLORP

Oog.

POKE!

Stop that! Ow! I am sick of this lousy dimension!
What is that, a mystical sword? It's useless without the secret symbols. Gimme.

Writing upside down is hard.

GOODBYEEEE!
VASHOOM!
Snop

SsssSSsssss
NASA
CRUNCH
POP

NASA
Did I get him?

I did, didn't I?
WOO!

Pirate Penguin! Nice aim! What were the chances of that?!?
One in seven.

I saved the day! Go me!

I helped! It was me with the sword! We make a good team.

Yes, I do make a good team!

Well, it's good to have you back! I missed ya buddy!!

I missed you too... kinda!

Hug?
No hugs.

Hey, you guys! Look what I found! It's part of that shiny sword, it broke off on the monster!
Ooh! Dibs!
Don't be selfish! I want the whole thing! I vanquished the monster. It was Pirate Penguin, to the left temple, with the spaceship!
Hold on, I helped! That's as much my claim as it is yours.

Nuh uh!!
Gimme!
FIGHT FIGHT FITE!
Rawr!

It was my idea to use the sword. I overheard the crucial line of dialogue that helped save the day.
I think I should keep the sword hilt.
Finders equal Keepers. Are they gonna be at this fight long? I already have a lunch appointment scheduled with Ninja Chicken.

Hmm, no, looks like they'll be at it a while. I'm getting pretty hungry too. Hey Squiddie, wanna get some lunch with me instead?
Um, geez, well... I was really hoping for Ninja Chicken. He's my flavorite.

Guess what?
Ninja Chicken is my favorite too!
BEEP!

FRIENDSHIP!
Let's talk about him for hours!
Yay!

ENEMYITUDE!!
SLAP! SLAP
SLAP!

Hey, where'd my spaceship go? Don't tell me I lost another one!
Mogu podkinut' tebia do Moskvi, no ostatok puti do doma tebe pridetsia dobiratsia avtostopom. Plus, na benzin skidivaemsia porovnu. Ladi?
*I can give you a lift as far as Moscow, but you'll have to hitchhike the rest of the way home. Plus, we go splitsies for gas. Okay-groovy?
THE END

Dangit! I think I left my keys in that other dimension. I hate it when that happens!
THE END
again

Epilogue:

Pirate Penguin and Ninja Chicken stopped fighting once they got tired, and got some lunch at an all-you-can-eat-buffet that wasn't too smashed. Pirate Penguin sneakily crammed his hat full of cocktail shrimp for later.

Coincidentally, Camoflaugey Chameleon and Ninja Squid were sitting at the next table over, loudly discussing the formation of their Ninja Chicken Fan Club. Totally embarassed, Ninja Chicken hid in the bathroom, while Pirate Penguin practiced his burping.

Astronaut Armadillo made it home safely, to find planet earth had been conqured by apes. But they were nice enough apes, and he was later sent on a mission to Mars that turned out to be a practical joke.

Parrot and Puppy from the beginning of the book are having a wonderful time on Super Candy Adventure Island, though they both have slight tummy aches from too much adventure candy.

The lobsters who stole Ninja Chicken's car were arrested hundreds of miles away on suspicion of pinching. They were found guilty/delicious.

Pirate Penguin and Ninja Chicken lost a buncha money on nickel black-jack, and had to ride the bus home from Las Vegas. Pirate Penguin's hat smelled very, very bad by the time they reached wherever it is they live.

THE ENDINGEST END

(UNTIL BOOK TWO)

ACTIVITIES!

Hello! Welcome to the activities section of the book! Here's some stuff for you to do! Ready? Go!

How to Make a Pirate Hat

1. Get a piece of paper.
1½. A BLANK piece of paper. A big one, too. The bigger the paper, the bigger the hat will be.
2. Fold it in half, in a folding-wise way.
3. Fold the top corners down toward the center of the page, so it looks like a sailboat.
4. Lift the bottom flaps up, so that it looks kinda like a pirate hat now.
5. Wear! In the right kind of light, your head will glow.
6. Customize! Draw pictures, color, add feathers and glitter and stuff to your hat!
7. (optional) draw beards and mustaches on your face if you want to TOTALLY look like a pirate.
8. Get in trouble, take a punishment bath, and then realize you used permanent marker, and that the stuff you drew is STUCK ON YOUR FACE FOREVER. OH NO!

How to Draw Pirate Penguin (The Quick Method)

1. Close your eyes, grab a pen and paper, and GO FOR IT! This does not always turn out perfectly.)

How to Draw Pirate Penguin (The Geometric method)

1. Draw A Triangle
2. Draw more triangles, some squares, and even a circle or two.
3. Fill in the details until it's Pirate Penguin shaped.

Ninja Chicken's Extra Hard SuDontKu

	3							
			7					

How to Make a Pair of Nunchuks

1. Get two rolls of paper towels.
2. Spill a bunch of soup and soda on the floor, then wipe it up. Use the whole roll so, you are left with nothing but the brown tube inside (or be a nice person, and wait till the roll is used up naturally, rather than making a mess.)
3. Using a pokey thing (such as a pencil or unicorn) poke a small hole in the bottom area of each cardboard tube.
4. Get a bunch of paperclips.
5. Smoongle them together into a big paperclip chain (this will require some smoongling. Make sure you wear your smoongle-shoes)
6. Smoongulate the paperclips, so that the end of each chain goes through one of the tube holes, and so now the paper towel tubes are clipped together.
7. Pose dramatically. Spin your nunchuks around. Any lamps or faces you break will be Your Problem. Sometimes the paperclips come undone, and the nunchuks will explode (but that really only makes them cooler).

Here's a pile of guest drawings a bunch of my friends (and a few of my enemies) made for me!
Heather Lawther
Beth Slevin
AVAST YE CUPCAKE!
Guy Davis
James Turner
TheUncle2k
Falynn Koch
Eugene "jJar"
Michael Spiers
Grace of Bass
SO COLD IT'S AAARGH-TIC!
Katie Cook
Gregg Schigiel
Chris Houghton
Chelsea "Not Quite Normal" Gordon-Ratzlaff
Crystal Chesney-Thompson
Derek Thompson

Dan "Wonderdookie" Barrett
Johane "Rufftoon" Matte
Michelle
"Owlcorns"
Harshberger
Beth Slevin
again
AARRR!
Roger
Langridge
NURSE!
HE'S OUT
OF BED
AGAIN
Karen Weiss
Kendraw
Cook
Rheebus
Bridget "Bon Bon Bunny" Garofalo
Thanks everybody! It's so cool seeing your characters in a different style.

OUTRODUCTION BY RAY FRIESEN

TROUBLEMS with FRENEMIES